Grandma vs. Zombies

Kicking Zombie Butt..."Old School" Style!

J.B. O'Neil

Grandma vs. Zombies

Kicking Zombie Butt..."Old School" Style!

Table of Contents

Thanks to Sam Boyer and John S. Rhodes for all of their fantastic ideas & invaluable help with these Family Avengers books.

And of course, many thanks to Eric Maruscak for his amazing illustrations and cover design.

FREE BONUS – Grandma vs. Zombies Audiobook!

Hey gang...If you'd like to listen to an audiobook version of "Grandma vs. Zombies" while you follow along with this book, you can download it for free for a limited time by going online and copying this link:

http://familyavengers.com/zombies/

Chapter 1: The Family Secret

My name is Jimmy Beezer. I'm ten years old. Last week, I made a model volcano in science class, got to eat pizza for lunch two days in a row at school, and then went on a trip with my family to Germany to blow up a factory that had been forced to produce an army of tiny laser-shooting robots built to destroy the world.

It was a cool weekend, but I missed my favorite TV show since it doesn't get on German TV. Also I didn't get to miss any school, so I had to take my math test on Monday like I was supposed to. Sometimes being a part of the world's most dangerous family really stinks...but mostly, it's awesome!

We're called The Family Avengers, a secret organization that was started by my great-grandparents almost a hundred years ago. Combining ancient martial arts and wisdom, modern extreme training, and advanced technology that makes sci-fi look like the stone age, The Family Avengers stands against giant angry sea monsters, aliens from outer space, swarms of super-intelligent bee people, armies of mind-controlled mutants, and mad (and crazy!) scientists trying to turn the Earth into one of Jupiter's moons!

In other words, we protect the world from stuff no one else can handle. It's a lot of fun, but it's pretty hard work, and come to think of it, I've never once gotten out of a math test for doing it. I guess I should study for them, or else I'm going to get in trouble when my report card shows up...

Chapter 2: The Afternoon of the Day the Living Dead Died Again

Me, my big sister Buffy, and my baby sister Baby (I guess my parents got lazy?) are the youngest members of The Family Avengers. We don't get to go on missions alone because we're just kids, but we still get to kick butt on weekends as long as we do our chores and get to bed on time!

But usually, we have to do our homework and go to school while the grow-ups fight evil. We always get to hear about what happened though, and hearing about the stories is still pretty cool.

Like the time Grandma Beezer destroyed a giant outbreak of zombies! I had always thought that Grandma was too old and nice to be part of The Family Avengers, but after seeing her come home and track zombie brains all over her fuzzy carpet with her motorcycle boots (and getting really mad about it when she found out), I totally get why my dad gets REALLY quiet whenever we visit her! Grandma Beezer is the coolest Grandma ever, and this is my favorite story about her...here's what happened.

That day, our parents were called by the United Nations to deal with some dumb monster that got lost on the way to Tokyo and had started eating Hawaii instead. My sister and I had already gotten blacklisted by every babysitter in town (because just ONE TIME we left the door to the Danger Room open...didn't he see it was called the "Danger Room?"), so our parents had to take us to Grandma's house in the Family Avenger's helicopter. Buffy had really wanted to pet the monster, but I was glad we didn't go. Anything international involved a lot of talking to worried people in suits, and I'm not allowed to play any video games while that's happening.

It was fun hanging out with Grandma, but also a little boring. She made us cookies, but they were too hard to eat (after they soaked in milk for an hour we could break them if we used a hammer). She didn't have any TV or even internet in her house, so she just let us look at her photo albums or play outside in the backyard. The best part was hearing about all the stuff she did when she was young; even now that she's 87, and isn't as strong or fast as she used to be, she still keeps ready for anything!

Chapter 3: Zombies!

Me and Buffy were sitting in the living room playing with Grandma's cats, while she sat outside in her rocking chair taking a nap. Suddenly, we heard loud crashes, followed by screaming!

Me and Buffy combat-rolled over to the windows just like we'd been practicing in field training all week, and slowly peeked out through the corners of the pink frilly blinds. We saw that the neighbor's house was surrounded by people, but something was a little funny about them. They slouched around and seemed to bump into each other a lot, and their clothes were all ripped up and dirty. They smelled like day-old barf on the lunch room floor. It wasn't until one of their arms suddenly fell off and thumped onto the ground that we realized that these weren't just neighbors with serious personal-hygiene issues...they were zombies!

We quietly made our way to Grandma on the front porch as fast as we could. She had her head tilted back, and she was snoring a little. Her false teeth were sitting on the table next to her.

"Grandma, wake up!" me and Buffy whispered.

Grandma snorted and her eyes fluttered open. "Wha, huh? I was just resting my eyes," she said.

"Grandma, you have to be quiet, there are zombies eating your neighbors!"

"WHAT?" Grandma said, cupping a hand over her ear and leaning towards us.

"SSH! Grandma, not so loud, or the zombies will hear!" Buffy whispered, glancing behind her at what looked like a hoard of the living dead pouring into the cul-de-sac from the road.

"YOU HAVE TO SPEAK UP BUFFY, AND NO, THERE ARE NO MONKEYS IN CLOWN GEAR AROUND HERE, DON'T BE SILLY!"

"No Grandma, the zombies! Zombies are here!" we started to point frantically at the slouching masses, which had now definitely noticed Grandma's shouting and were stumbling in our direction.

Grandma squinted at where we were pointing, patted around for her glasses for a really long time, and then finally put them on. "Ohh, I see now. Zombies in the neighborhood. I told the town council that holding the hog-calling competition right next to the graveyard was a bad idea, but they never listen to me until it's too late."

"Grandma, we have our gadgets here! We can help you fight them!" Buffy said.

"No no no dearies, you're going to have to get inside and stay put. Zombies are much too dangerous for anyone without experience, and I don't want to have to explain to your mother and father that I had to blow your heads off with a shotgun because you got bitten by one of those things! Now run along: I know how to take care of this."

Chapter 4: Grandma Cowboy's Up

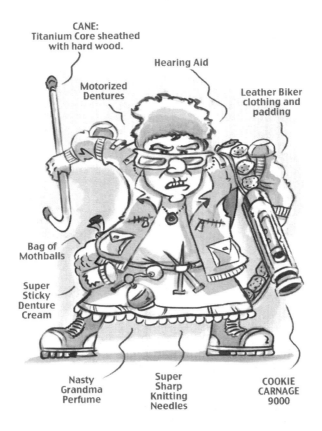

CANE:
Titanium Core sheathed with hard wood.

Hearing Aid

Motorized Dentures

Leather Biker clothing and padding

Bag of Mothballs

Super Sticky Denture Cream

Nasty Grandma Perfume

Super Sharp Knitting Needles

COOKIE CARNAGE 9000

We didn't want to stay in the house and read boring issues of "Knitting and Napping Weekly," but Grandma wouldn't hear of it and she pushed us back inside the house. "Don't you worry kids," she said as she walked into her bedroom, "I've been dealing with zombies since they were in black-and-white! You just have to know how to deal with those walking stink-bags. You kids stay put, I'm gearing up to kick some zombie butt!"

When grandma came back out of her bedroom, she was in full Zombie Killing Family Avengers Mode! Her weapons of choice:

-Her cane, a titanium core sheathed with hard wood!

-Her motorized dentures

-Her super-sticky denture cream

-A bag of mothballs

-A bottle of her thickest, strongest perfume

-Her trusty sharp knitting needles

-And her favorite weapon of all: The Cookie Carnage 9000, a devastating fully-automatic machine gun capable of firing 700 CPM (cookies per minute) at an accurate range of 300 yards.

Grandma also had:

-Her hearing aid, which carries a special button inside that Grandma only uses in emergencies

-Studded leather biker gear, which does a great job of protecting from Zombie bites, scratches, and road rash if she has to dump her....

-Motorcycle! Grandma ruled the roads back in the day and still does now with this old-school chopper!

Lastly, Grandma has a secret weapon, like any good member of The Family Avengers: her old creepy doll collection (me and Buffy never go into their room). They look like they could start moving on their own...

Chapter 5: The Zombie's Powers

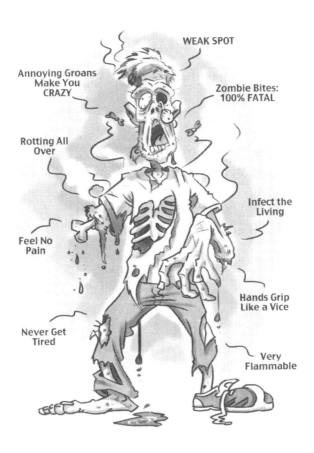

WEAK SPOT

Annoying Groans Make You CRAZY

Zombie Bites: 100% FATAL

Rotting All Over

Infect the Living

Feel No Pain

Hands Grip Like a Vice

Never Get Tired

Very Flammable

Those zombies were more than just ugly and dumb (but mostly, they're ugly and dumb). Here's what the zombies had to put up a fight against Grandma:

-Their stiff hands can grip you like a vise, and they never, ever let go of what they grab until they've eaten it!

-Their teeth are broken, loose, and razor-sharp. Plus, if they bite you, you'll turn into one!

-As everyone knows, zombies can only be killed in one of two ways: destroying their brain, or burning them with fire!

-They don't feel pain, probably because they're too stupid. Cut off a leg, break their nose...none of that makes any difference because they'll keep coming after you!

-Their moaning and groaning can paralyze humans with fear and distract even the best warriors. Some say that if you listen long enough it will drive you crazy!

-Their decaying flesh is disgusting and rotting away, so the smell is HORRIBLE!

The fact that zombie bites are 100% fatal and contagious makes them a constant threat to the world. In fact, one famous scientist calculated that a single zombie can infect 8 normal humans every hour. If each of those 8 new zombies each infected 8 more humans, then in less than half a day, the entire world would become zombified! It's simply math.

Zombies are considered a Class 4 threat by The Family Avengers, at least if they get out of control. Even Baby Beezer could probably fend off a single zombie just by distracting it with her rattle...they're that stupid. But get them in any kind of group, and they're really dangerous.

Grandma had a lot of guts to fight a big group of them by herself...end of story.

Chapter 6: Hells' Oldest Angel

Grandma got on her chopper and gunned the throttle. The explosive rumble drew the rotten eyes of every zombie in the neighborhood, but that was just fine with Grandma. She liked the fight to come to her!

"YEEHAH! Let's tango you zonked-out creeps!" Grandma cried, and zoomed forward into the thickest part of the hoard. This was the only part that Sis and I got to see, since we were stuck looking out the window, but it sure beat TV!

Grandma crashed into the first group of zombies like a bowling ball. They flew everywhere, and Grandma's bike was so heavy a lot of the zombies ended up exploding into little pieces! Then Grandma pulled out her cane and started whacking zombies in the head, smashing their heads open like rotten watermelons, and the bits flew out so hard they knocked other zombies over. Somehow, Grandma managed to run over the head of every zombie that fell down, shouting "anyone for brain casserole? Come and get it!"

Of course, the zombies were too dumb to realize they were getting creamed by Grandma and her bike. They just kept on stumbling toward Grandma wherever she went, and that was part of her plan all along: she wasn't just having fun, she was luring the zombies away from the neighborhood! She quickly put together a long tail of zombies that clumsily followed her up the street and out of sight.

From then on, I just had to hear about it from Grandma when she got back. But Grandma's a really good story-teller, so it felt like I was right there the whole time.

Chapter 7: Slow and Steady Wins the Race

Even though Grandma likes sleeping and knitting when she's not on duty, she's probably the craziest Family Avenger when she gets the chance. The cars parked along the side of the road made excellent ramps for Grandma!

She nailed every jump as she tore down the street, pulling off a few flips when she felt like it. When she knew she was too far ahead she doubled back down the entire mile-long parade of zombies, cracking a few skulls with her cane as she went and teasing the zombies. I guess she said a lot of cuss-words too, but Grandma wouldn't tell me about them.

Grandma had a lot of fun, but she slapped her forehead when the bike started to sputter. She had forgotten to check the gas tank and was going to have to pull over and take care of these zombies on foot.

Luckily Grandma had gotten through the town and was out in the country. She spotted an old abandoned farmhouse near the road, so she jumped off her bike at 60 miles an hour, rolling on the ground. She stood up, turned around to face the zombies, and shouted "Hey you mush-brains! I'm over here! Don't you want to taste this tough piece o' jerky? MY Grandma could outrun you and she's been dead longer than most of you have!"

The zombies shuffled after Grandma, and she ducked into the farmhouse. Grandma was going to fight the zombies for real now: play-time was over!

Chapter 8: Usable On All Pests

As soon as Grandma had gotten well inside the farmhouse, she reached inside her jacket and pulled out her giant sack of mothballs. "I hope they have a nice trip," Grandma giggled, dropping the mothballs all over the floor. Then she got out her cane again, and stood just out of sight.

The zombies started to shuffle inside the old farmhouse. There were so many of them they clogged up the door, even though it was twenty feet wide!

Not one of them saw the mothballs spread all over the dirt floor.

The first zombie stepped right on top of one, slipped, and suddenly the zombies were falling like dominoes, some smashing their heads together so hard they killed each-other! One slipped on so many mothballs it rolled all the way across the farmhouse to a window, crashed through it, and fell down a hill. Grandma checked on it later, and it had gone so fast and fallen so hard it had been turned into Zom-bits.

"HALLELUIA!" Grandma cried, and she started cracking zombie heads so fast and hard it sounded like a thunderstorm. Crash! Bang! Boom! It was so loud we heard it back at Grandma's house!

After she had killed about fifty zombies, the door wasn't so clogged anymore and the zombies started swarming for real. Grandma moved like she was late for the early-bird special at the Cubby Hole Diner! She got out her bottle of disgusting, smelly perfume and threw it at the ground, making a big thick purple cloud of perfume-fog rise up and blind the zombies! Then she slipped silently behind an old tractor and made her way to the back of the barn, like the ninja that she was.

Chapter 9: What's That Sonny?

The zombies moped around looking for Grandma, but all they found were more mothballs to kill themselves with. Grandma was hiding behind a big bale of hay in the back of the farmhouse, trying to let as many zombies file in as she could. They were moving so slowly that they were still coming in from the road! But as the farmhouse filled up with the stumbling dead, their moaning got louder, and louder, and LOUDER.

Zombie moaning can quickly drive people crazy because it never, ever stops. Grandma is a Family Avenger, so of course she wasn't worried about that. Luckily for her, she was almost deaf already! Grandma reached into her ear and turned her hearing aid off to completely silence the horrible zombie wails.

'Now it's time to Rock n' Roll!,' Grandma thought to herself. She popped her big old dentures out of her mouth and pushed a small button hidden in one of the molars. Then she tossed the teeth over the hay and into the middle of the zombies.

As soon as the teeth landed they began to shudder, chatter, jump and hop all around. The zombies immediately turned to face the shiny chattering teeth, and crowded together to try to grab them. These dead dummies were all squashed together, bumping and shoving each another to get at the noisy teeth, and they forgot all about Grandma.

But Grandma didn't forget about them!

Chapter 10: Have a Cookie!

While the zombies were stupidly swarming around her false teeth, Grandma had had plenty of time to load up her favorite zombie-killing weapon!

She pivoted out from behind the haystack, and her riding scarf was now tied over her head like a bandanna. "I baked cookies! Who wants some!?" Grandma cried, and squeezed the trigger of the Cookie Carnage 9000!

Grandma laughed out loud as her rock-hard oatmeal cookies of doom tore into the zombie horde. "Eat this suckers!" she screamed.

The zombies tried to make their way to Grandma, but she kept pouring on cookies at full automatic, splattering their heads so hard they looked like fireworks! Brains, bones, ears and rotten eyeballs flew everywhere while Grandma grinned and fired away!

Grandma had come with almost a thousand cookies on her, but the Cookie Carnage 9000 ran out of cookies before the zombies ran out of heads. The farmhouse floor was covered in zombie parts nearly two feet deep, but now Grandma was trapped behind this pile of stinking zombie meat and couldn't get out!

Chapter 11: Enemy's Everywhere!

"OK you losers, you've put me in a tricky spot again," Grandma sneered. She cracked her knuckles and grabbed her cane. "Let's dance!" she said, and jumped right in the middle of the remaining group of zombies.

Grandma whirled and twirled, punching zombies so hard she knocked their heads off and sent them flying into the rafters of the old barn! Those were the lucky ones; any zombie that got hit with her cane may as well have gotten hit by a bomb. She was smashing her way through the crowd, but realized something was wrong. There were just too many zombies! They were grabbing her arms and legs, slowing her down just a little too much. One zombie even managed to bite her leather jacket, but luckily it didn't have any teeth left thanks to Grandma's vicious cane attack.

Grandma loved that jacket, but she loved living even more. The zombie wouldn't let go, so she wiggled out of the jacket and retreated, kicking at the zombies grabbing her feet and crushing them like juicy bugs. One zombie bit down on her cane and wrenched it out of her grip, but she broke through the crowd just in time. Grandma was back where she started, but she didn't have her cane!

"OK, now you've made me mad," Grandma growled. "That was my favorite jacket, and you ate it!" The zombies didn't listen though. They were closing in!

Chapter 12: One of Us! One of Us!

The tips of the zombie's fingers were brushing against Grandma's old-lady blouse. "This is a sticky situation," Grandma said, "so it'll take something even stickier to get me out of it!"

She got out her jar of sticky denture cream, rubbing it onto her hands and the soles of her boots. She put her hands and feet on the wall and climbed straight up it like a spider! It was such a close call one of the zombies pulled off one of her riding boots, but suddenly she was safe!

Grandma breathed a sigh of relief as she hung from the side of the barn wall, then started thinking about her next move. "All out of cookies, they got my cane, and this sticky cream won't stick for long..." she muttered. "Guess I gotta pull out the big guns. It's too bad really, I wanted to give those dolls to my darling grandchildren..."

"...but I'll just make sure to knit them an extra Christmas sweater this year!"

(Doh!)

Chapter 13: The Kamikaze Doll Squadron Arrives

The zombies turned around when they heard the scream of jet engines, and through the door flew Grandma's entire collection of creepy dolls, flying on rockets!

"Play with us!" the dolls squealed in their tiny voices, their beady little eyes shining and their faces smiling. The dolls smashed themselves into the zombies, creating tiny explosions and blowing zombies to pieces. "Play with us! Play with us!" The dolls screamed, and the zombies moaned and groaned, swiping at dolls and completely missing every time. One zombie managed to catch a doll and bite it, but the doll exploded and blew the top of the zombie's head off!

"Go my pretties! Kill, kill!" Grandma screamed.

When the last doll had blown itself up, there were only about a dozen zombies left. "It's payback time! Gimme back my cane!" Grandma cried, and she leapt off the wall, landing on both feet. Then she pulled out her two trusty knitting needles...

Chapter 14: 1,000 Stitches of Death!

"Time for you crud-buckets to see what happens when you mess with Grandma Beezer! Here comes my 1,000 Stitches of Death!"

Grandma started moving so fast she became a blur, knitting the zombies together! She knit hair to knees, arms to heads, and mouths to butts! For good measure Grandma poked the eyes out of all the zombies with her super-sharp knitting needles, bursting them like grapes. Wriggling maggots dropped out of the sockets and onto the floor, where they were probably really happy for a while because of all the zombie parts there!

In just a few seconds, Grandma had made a big moaning pile of blind, tied-together zombies. They tried to move, but all they could do was wave their arm-heads around and moan into their butts. Except for those, there were no zombies left!

Chapter 15: BBQ Flavor

Now Grandma had to clean up. "I gotta take care of this mess, but I'm feeling a little tired now...I bet no one will miss this old shack."

Grandma fished around inside her blouse and got out her trusty old lighter, and flicked up a flame. She lit up the bales of hay scattered all over of the barn, and within seconds fire was cheerfully roasting the zombies.

"Whoops, nearly forgot my cane," Grandma said, slowly prying a zombie hand still wrapped around her #1 weapon. She brushed off her blouse, then started whistling as she walked out of the burning barn.

The barn was completely burned to the ground by the time the police and firefighters arrived, and grandma was already walking her motorcycle back up the road and heading for home.

"Zombie attack boys! Haven't seen that many in 27 years," Grandma cackled, swatting the police sergeant on the back. "Sure is lucky they came around my neck of the woods, or we would've had a full-on zombie outbreak! Any chance of a gallon of gas for the ol' hog?"

"S-sure thing ma'am," the sergeant said. "I c-c-can't believe you're still working!"

"Better believe it now sonny, I'm still not too old to put down a zombie hoard! I'll let you clean this up. Tell Police Chief Halliburton to send me the paperwork whenever he gets around to it."

The police never liked having to clean up after Grandma Beezer, but they all agreed: they were really glad that Grandma was still kicking butt...Family Avengers Style!

Chapter 16: That's Our Grandma

Me and Buffy had heard all the explosions, and of course we couldn't miss the army of dolls launching out of the house and breaking all the windows as they jetted off to help Grandma at the barn, so of course we were expecting Grandma when she walked through the front door again 30 minutes later. That's when she tracked the zombie brains all over her white carpeting.

"Grandma, Grandma! How many were there? Did anyone get bitten?" we asked.

"Did anyone get bitten? Gosh darn kids, you don't really think I'd let that happen, do you?" Grandma said as she washed off her slimy knitting needles in the kitchen sink.

"No Grandma..." we said.

"Well, don't ask such a silly question then, dearies. Now I need to get back to knitting your sweater, Jimmy," Grandma said, sitting down in her rocking chair and lifting up a half-finished green-and-purple sweater.

"Aw Grandma, not another turtleneck sweater!" I moaned, "The kids at school are STILL making fun of me for the last one!"

"You kids just don't get it: the old ways are the best ways!" Grandma said, picking up an oatmeal cookie from the tray on the table. She took a big bite, put it aside, and started to knit my Christmas present with the same needles that she had just used to pop out zombie eyeballs.

Yup, me and Buffy and Baby Beezer still have a LOT to learn in our training as the youngest Family Avengers...and we'll definitely NEVER roll our eyes again when Grandma starts talking about the "good old days" of bad-guy butt-kicking.

THE END

Sneak Peak: Jimmy Vs. Vampires

Check out this exciting excerpt from my next book in the Family Avengers, Jimmy vs. Vampires!

I tip-toed over to the coffin. It looked like it was made of something heavy, like marble or stone. The lid would be really heavy…but I can do a hundred pushups, so I didn't think it'd be a problem.

I heaved at the lid and it slowly moved, grinding and groaning like a fat guy getting rolled out of bed. It wasn't long before I was panting and sweating, but I finally got the lid far enough that it did the rest of the work for me and crashed off the coffin base.

I looked inside, and there it was: the drifter vampire. It was a lady vampire, with long black hair and smooth, pale skin. She looked like she was sleeping, but I knew better. If I watched carefully I wouldn't see her breathe, and if I listened, I would not hear her heart beat. Vampires are dead, and when they hide from the sun, they act like it.

My mouth was dry as I brought up my Louisville stake-bat and placed the sharp spike right over the monster's heart.

For a minute I just stood there with the stake sitting on the vampire's chest. I had seen vampires get staked in the movies, and I knew from all my homework that a staked vampire just turns into dust, but still…I was a little scared. And I'm not afraid to admit it.

Using both hands, I lifted the stake up, then brought it down sharply to put the evil creature to rest forever.

Clawed hands grabbed the stake less than an inch from the skin. And they also grabbed my arm.

"Silly little boy," I heard the vampire whisper as it pulled me down, "you were just a bit too slow."

More Books by J.B. O'Neil

Hi gang! I hope you liked "Grandma vs. Zombies." Here are some more funny books I've written that I think you'll like too...

http://jjsnip.com/fart-book

And...

http://jjsnip.com/booger-fart-books

Silent but Deadly...As a Ninja Should Be!

http://jjsnip.com/ninja-farts-book

Did you know cavemen farted?

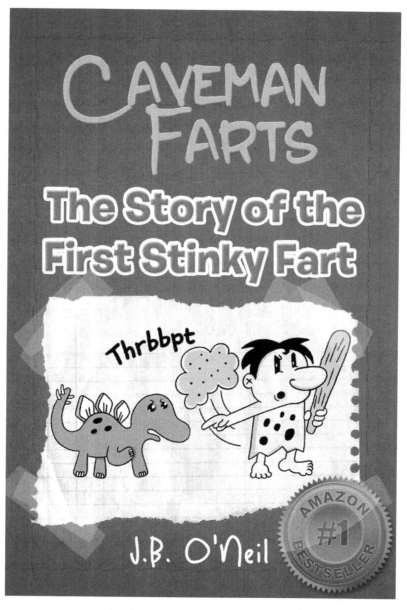

http://jjsnip.com/caveman-farts

Think twice before you blame the dog!

http://jjsnip.com/dog-farts

A long time ago, in a galaxy fart, fart away...

http://jjsnip.com/fart-wars

Made in the USA
Middletown, DE
18 June 2015